The Case of Piltdown

Contents

Written by Narinder Dhami

Illustrated by Eugene Smith

Collins

An astonishing scoop!

On a grey day in 1912, a fossil hunter came to Piltdown.

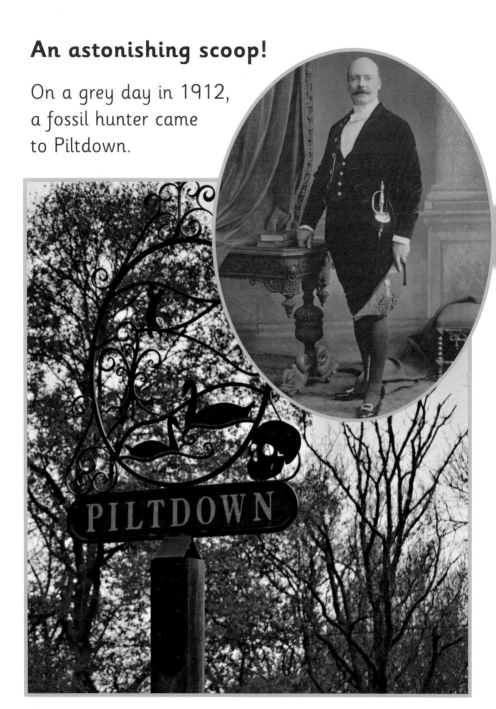

He wasn't a fossil expert by trade, but he had a keen interest in collecting them.

As he scraped and raked away the gravel, he came across fossil **fragments** in a **decaying** grave.

He gave them to a friend named Arthur, a fossil expert.

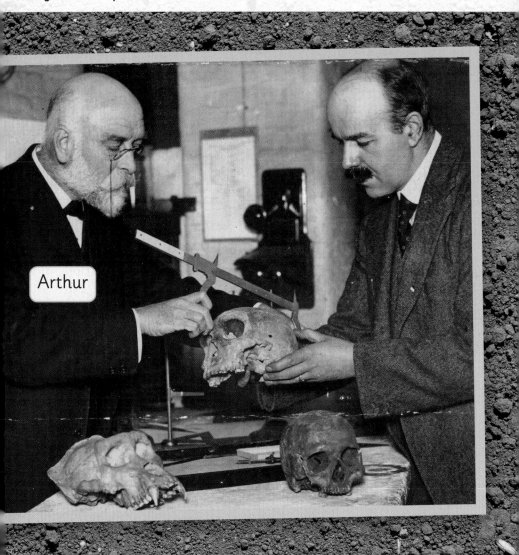

Arthur

The friends dug up fossils of a male skull and chin.

The fossils were named the Piltdown Man.
Arthur said they were all from the same
living thing.

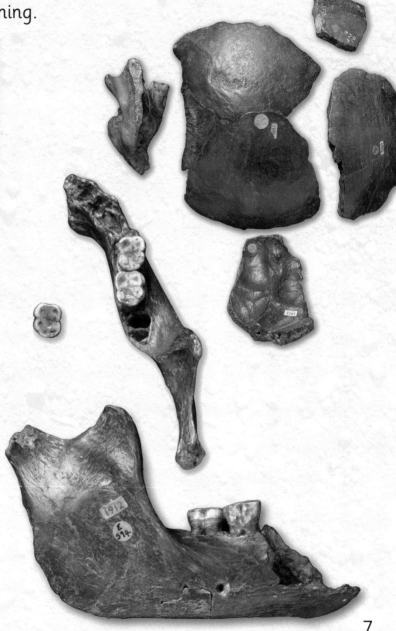

Important fossils

People and apes are related. However, fossils that linked apes and people had not been seen.

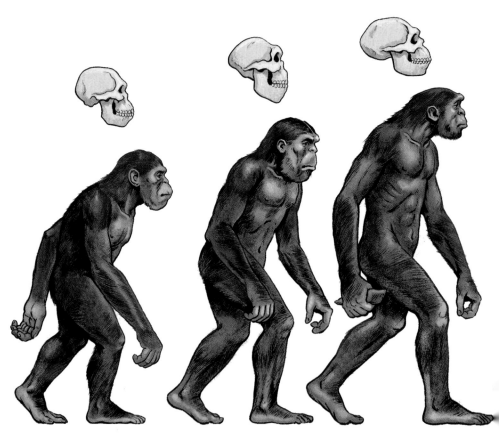

ape

Was the Piltdown Man this **missing link**?

person

The skull was shaped like a man's, but the chin was like an ape's chin.

Arthur estimated the fossils dated back 500,000 years. He fixed them up, then displayed them.

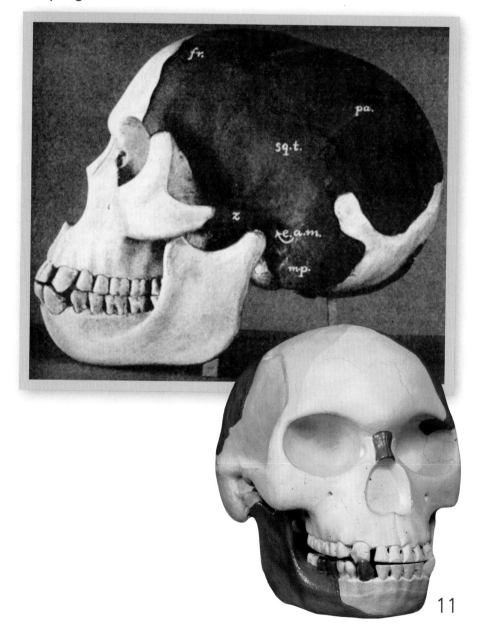

The Piltdown Man gained a lot of fame.

This is the missing link!

Missing link on display

Fake fossils

But right away, people suspected the Piltdown Man was fake.

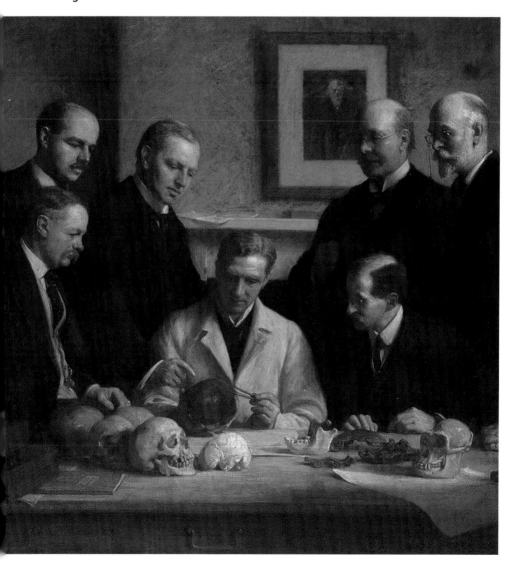

They said the fossils were not from the same living thing.

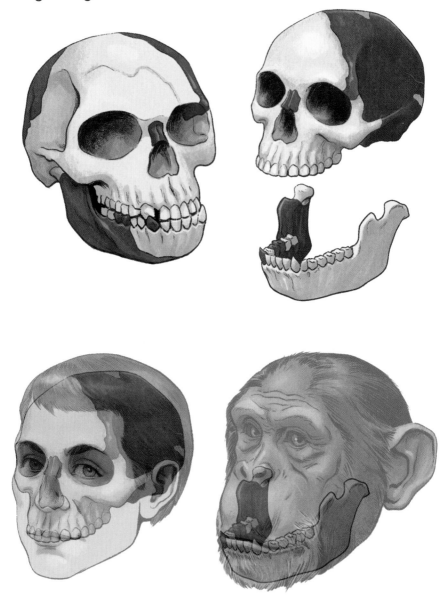

The fossil hunters felt full of dismay.

Have we been **taken in** by Piltdown Man?

Is Piltdown Man fake?

To **rein in** the gossip, Arthur shut the Piltdown fossils away in a safe.

But experts still kept discussing the Piltdown Man.

The proof

By 1949, interest in the Piltdown Man still hadn't faded away.

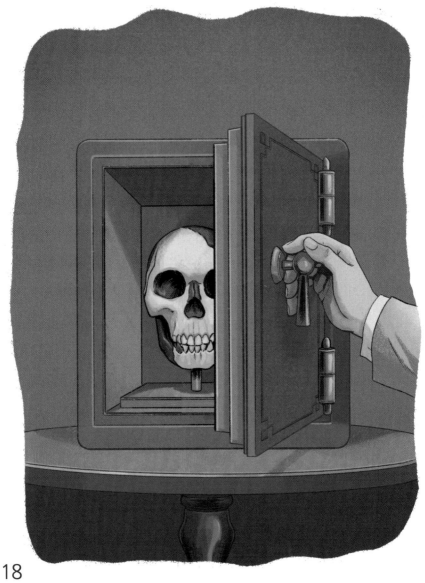

There were now modern ways to **date** fossils.

Some interesting points were soon raised ...

The Piltdown fossils did not date back as far as Arthur estimated.

Brown stains had been added, and the skull and chin were not from the same living thing.

In 1953, experts had proof that the Piltdown Man was a clever fake.

The suspects

People didn't hesitate to name Arthur as the man that faked the fossils.

However, a man named Martin Hinton hated Arthur and may have faked the fossils to shame him.

But lots of people blamed Arthur's friend, the fossil hunter.

He had cases full of
further fakes.
Was it him?

Nowadays, we still see fake things on screen. Perhaps the case of the Piltdown Man will alert us to fakes!

Glossary

date to estimate when a fossil is from

decaying getting worn out

fragments bits

missing link the link connecting things

rein in stop

taken in think a thing is correct

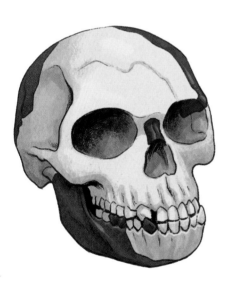

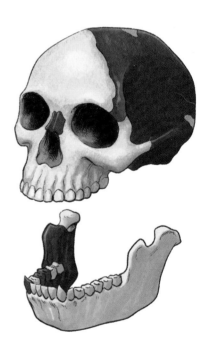

Index

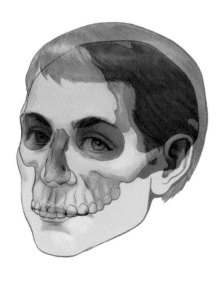
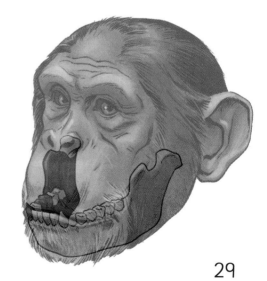

The important dates

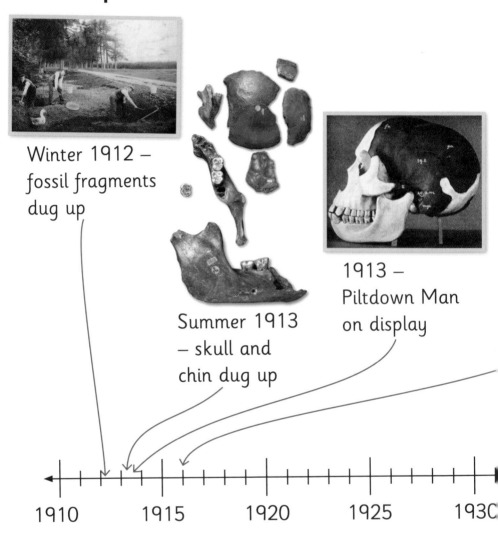

Winter 1912 –
fossil fragments
dug up

Summer 1913
– skull and
chin dug up

1913 –
Piltdown Man
on display

1910   1915   1920   1925   1930

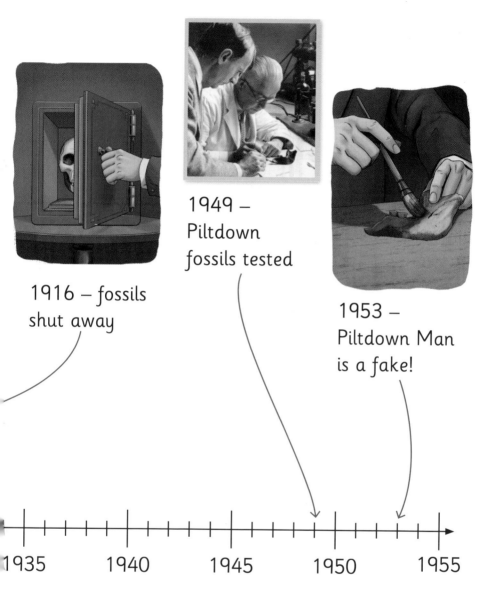

1916 – fossils
shut away

1949 –
Piltdown
fossils tested

1953 –
Piltdown Man
is a fake!

1935   1940   1945   1950   1955

 After reading

Letters and Sounds: Phase 5

Word count: 390

Focus phonemes: /ai/ ay, a-e, ey, ei

Common exception words: of, to, the, all, by, full, are, he, we, said, have, were, when, people, friend, like, there, was, some, what, wasn't

Curriculum links: Science: Evolution and inheritance

National Curriculum learning objectives: Reading/word reading: apply phonic knowledge and skills as the route to decode words; read accurately by blending sounds in unfamiliar words containing GPCs that have been taught; Reading/comprehension (KS2): understand what they read, in books they can read independently, by checking that the text makes sense to them, discussing their understanding and explaining the meaning of words in context; identifying main ideas drawn from more than one paragraph and summarising these

Developing fluency

- Take turns to read a page, demonstrating reading with expression and pausing for commas and full stops.
- Check your child does not miss reading the labels and uses a rising tone for questions.

Phonic practice

- Focus on words containing the /ai/ sound. Turn to page 13 and point to **away**. Ask your child to sound it out, then talk about how each letter "a" makes a different sound. (/a/ and /ai/).
- Ask your child to read the following words. Challenge them to identify the letters that make the /ai/ sound:
  fake (*a-e*) display (*ay*) they (*ey*) rein (*ei*) stains (*ai*) estimated (*a-e*)

Extending vocabulary

- Ask your child to explain the following words or phrases in the context they are used.
  page 3: by trade (e.g. *as paid work, as a profession*)
  page 15: full of dismay (e.g. *shocked, surprised and upset*)
  page 18: faded away (e.g. *disappeared, slowly gone away*)